SEB

For Amy 9,
With love
Grammy... March 1984

898

The
Yellow
Boat

The Yellow Boat

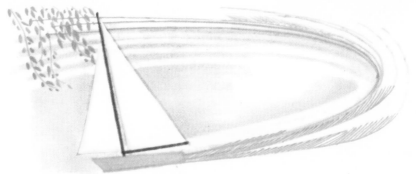

Margaret Hillert

Illustrated by Ed Young

 Follett Publishing Company   •   Chicago

Copyright © 1966, by Follett Publishing Company. All rights reserved. No part of this book may be reproduced in any form without written permission from the publisher. Manufactured in the United States of America.

Library of Congress Catalog Card Number: AC 66-10515

ISBN 0-695-39842-3 Paper edition
ISBN 0-695-49842-8 Library edition

Fourteenth Printing

6

Look here, look here.

See the little boat.

A little yellow boat.

The boat can go.

It can go away.

Go, little boat, go.

Away, away.

The boat can go away.

Oh, look, look.

Here is something.

It is funny.

Oh, my.

It can jump.

See it jump.

Jump, jump, jump.

Oh, oh, oh.

Something big is here.

Big, big, big.

Can it jump?

It can not jump.

It can go down, down, down.

Look here, look here.

One little one.

Two little ones.

Three little ones.

Where is the boat?

Where is it?

Find the little boat.

Oh, here it is.

Here is the yellow boat.

Go, boat, go.

Go away, away.

Here is something little.

It is blue.

It can go up.

Up, up, up and away.

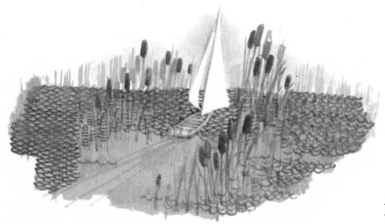

Here is a mother.

Here is a baby.

A little yellow baby.

20

Look, look.

See the baby play.

And here is something funny.

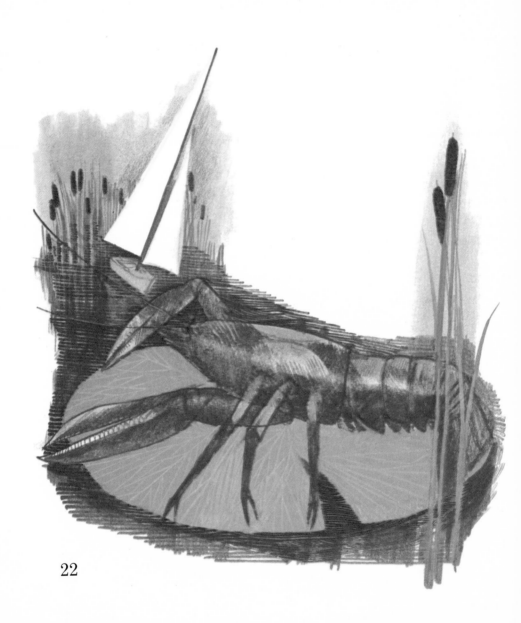

Help, help.

Go away, go away.

You make me want to run.

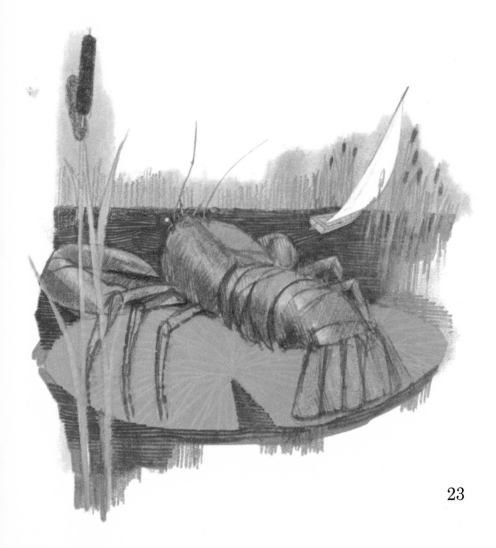

Here comes something.

I see something little.

Oh my, oh my.

It is a little yellow boat.

See the yellow boat.

Oh, yellow boat.

I want you.

I want you.

Come to my house.

Here you go.

In here, in here.

Go, yellow boat, go.

Follett JUST Beginning-to-Read Books

Uses of these books. These books are planned for the very youngest readers, those who have been learning to read for about six to eight weeks and who have a small preprimer reading vocabulary. The books are written by Margaret Hillert, a first-grade teacher in the Royal Oak, Michigan, schools. Each book is illustrated in full color.

Children will have a feeling of accomplishment in their first reading experiences with these delightful books that *they can read.*

The Yellow Boat

Children will enjoy the adventure of the yellow boat which is charmingly illustrated and uses just 43 preprimer words.

Word List

7	look		funny		baby
	here	**11**	my	**21**	play
	see		jump	**23**	help
	the	**12**	big		you
	little	**13**	not		make
	boat		down		me
	a	**14**	one		want
	yellow		two		to
8	can		three		run
	go	**15**	where	**24**	comes
	it		find		I
	away	**18**	blue	**26**	house
10	oh	**19**	up	**27**	in
	is		and		
	something	**20**	mother		